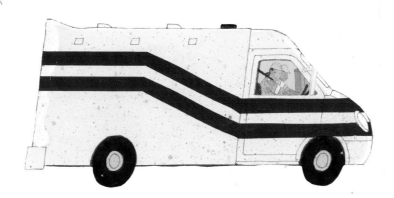

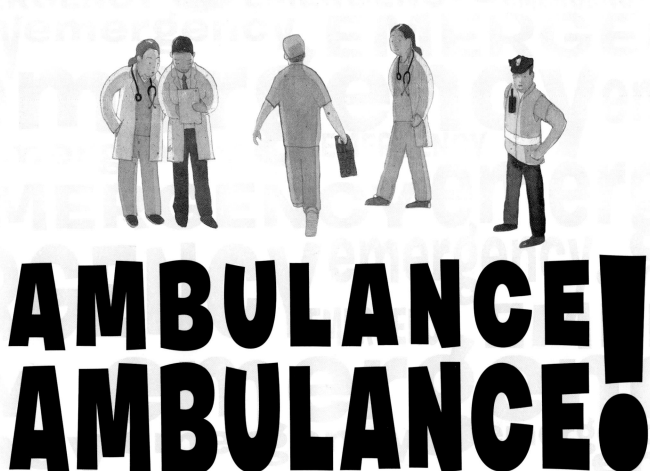

AMBULANCE! AMBULANCE!

SALLY SUTTON · ILLUSTRATED BY BRIAN LOVELOCK

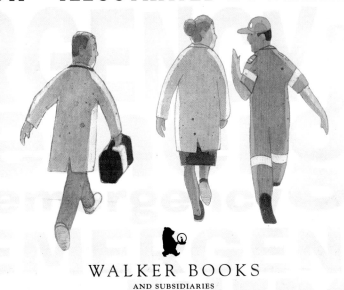

WALKER BOOKS

AND SUBSIDIARIES

LONDON · BOSTON · SYDNEY · AUCKLAND

Bleep, bleep. Emergency!
News just through:
Crash, crash, there's been a crash.
Let's go, crew!

Nee nar nee nar

nee nar nee nar...

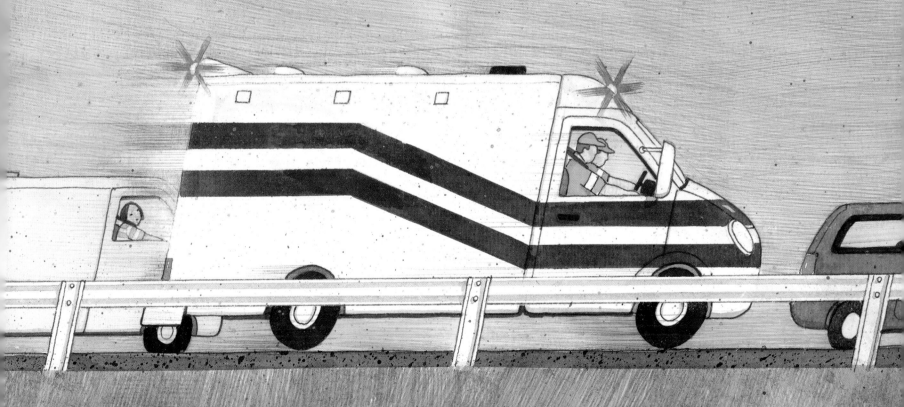

Stop, stop the ambulance.
Bump bump bump.
Grab, grab the rescue pack.
Out we jump.

Check, check the rider's heart.

Boom boom boom.

Splint, splint his broken leg.

Right! Let's zoom!

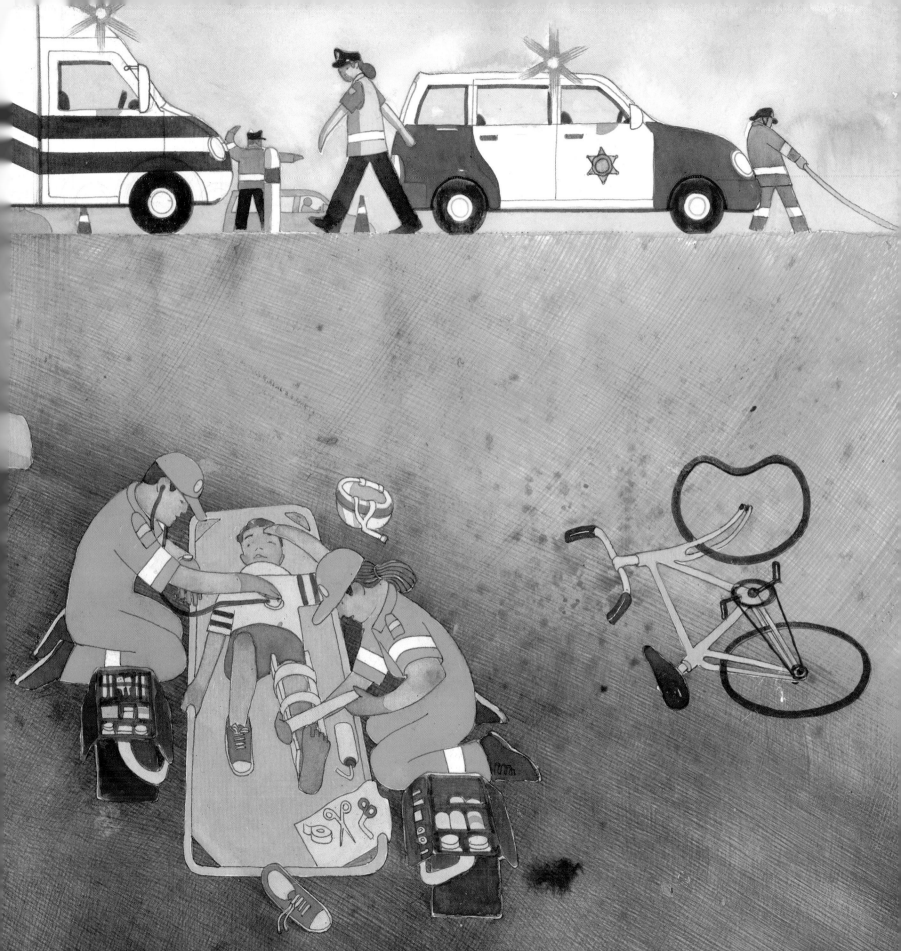

Lift, lift the stretcher in.
Slide and lock.
Call, call the hospital.
"Stand by, doc!"

Close, close the heavy doors.

Clink clank clonk.

Sound, sound the giant horn.

Honk honk honk!

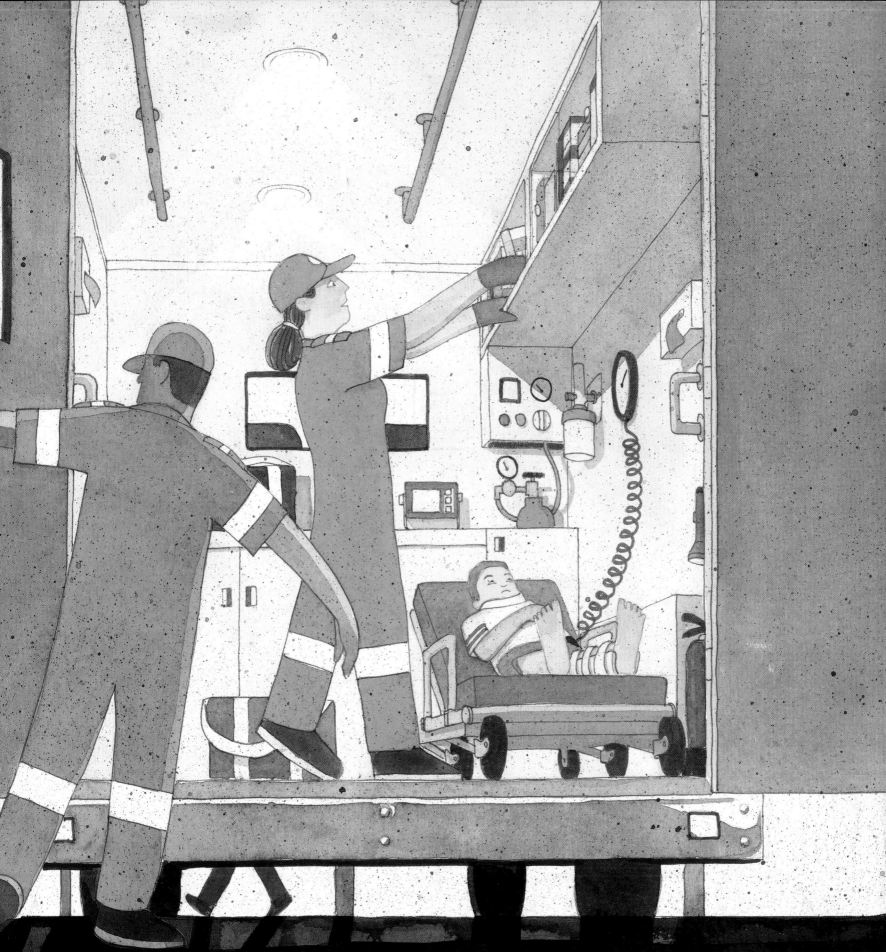

Flash, flash
the warning lights.
Flick flick flick.
Race, race to hospital.
Quick quick quick!

Nee nar nee nar

nee nar nee nar...

Wheel, wheel the patient in.
Teams crowd round.
Soon, soon he'll be fixed up.
Safe and sound.

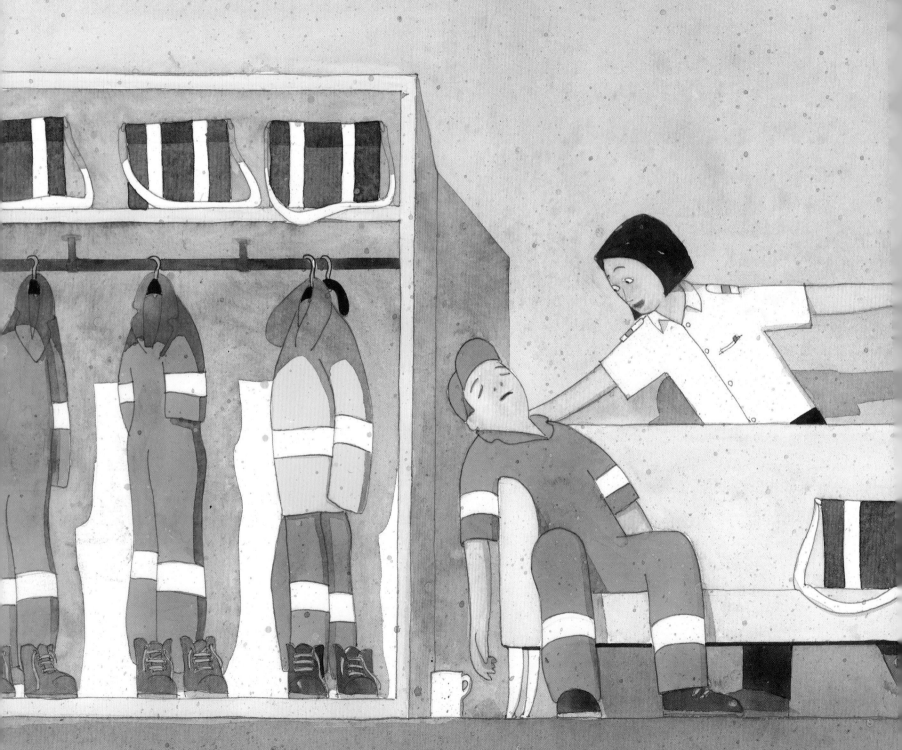

Phew, phew, let's take a break.
Then ... oh, no!
Bleep, bleep. Emergency!
Off we go ...

nee nar nee nar...

For Theo, and his most
excellent Grandpa. SS

For Harry. BL

First published 2017
by Walker Books Ltd,
87 Vauxhall Walk,
London SE11 5HJ

This edition published 2019

10 9 8 7 6 5 4 3 2 1

Text © 2017 Sally Sutton

Illustrations © 2017 Brian Lovelock

The right of Sally Sutton and Brian Lovelock to be identified as the author
and illustrator respectively of this work has been asserted by them in
accordance with the Copyright, Designs and Patents Act 1988

This book has been typeset in Burbank Big Regular

Printed in China

British Library Cataloguing in Publication Data:
a catalogue record for this book is available from the British Library

ISBN 978-1-4063-8085-9

www.walker.co.uk

Sally Sutton is the author of picture books *Roadworks*, *Demolition* and *Construction*, all illustrated by Brian Lovelock, and *Farmer John's Tractor*, illustrated by Robyn Belton. Sally lives in Auckland, New Zealand, with her husband and two daughters. Find her online at sallysutton.co.nz.

Brian Lovelock has painted all his life. A versatile artist, he particularly enjoys drawing people. His picture book titles include *Your Mother Didn't Do That!*, *The Rain Train*, *Roadworks*, *Demolition* and *Construction*. Brian lives in Auckland, New Zealand, with his wife and two children.

Also by Sally and Brian:

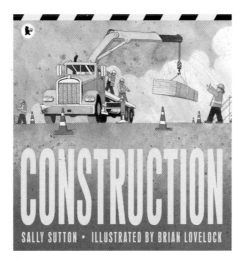

ISBN 978-1-4063-6715-7

Available from all good booksellers

www.walker.co.uk

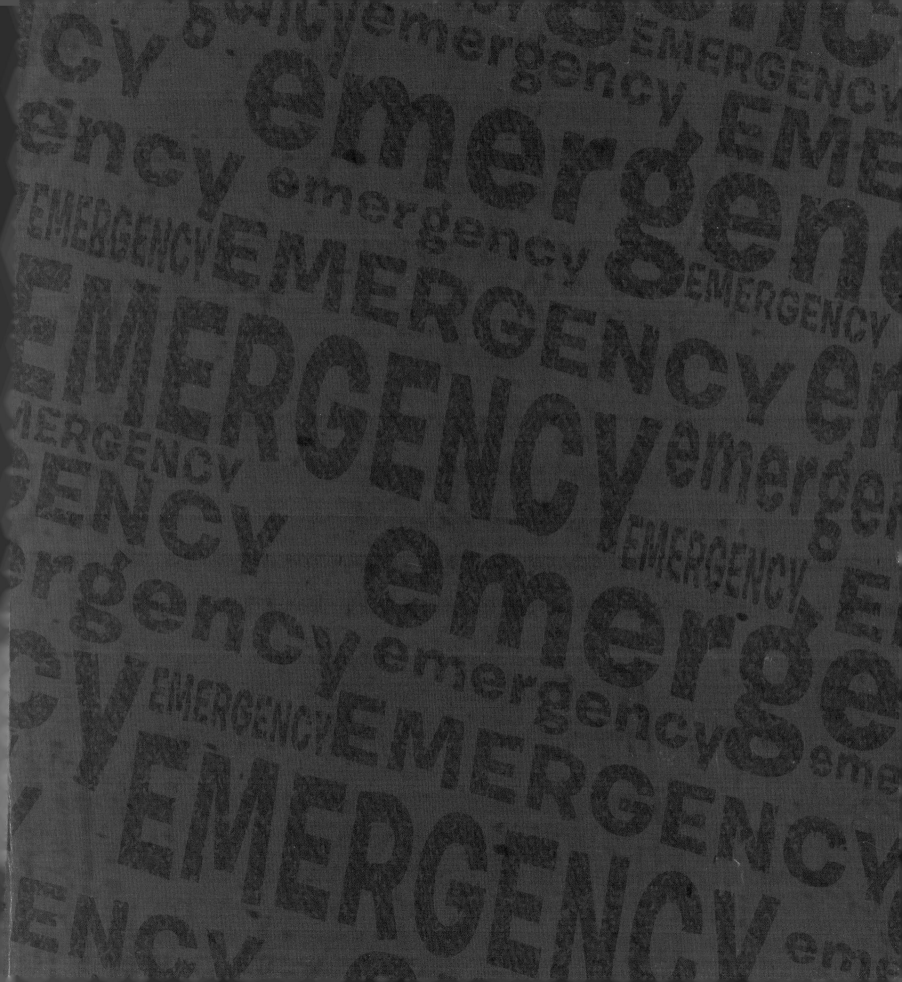